Yellow Umbrella Books are published by Capstone Press
151 Good Counsel Drive, P.O. Box 669, Mankato, Minnesota 56002
http://www.capstone-press.com

Library of Congress Cataloging-in-Publication Data
Ring, Susan.
  Light and shadow / by Susan Ring.
    p. cm.—(Science)
    Includes index.
  Summary: Introduces different kinds of light, the properties of light, and how light can create shadows of different shapes and sizes.
  ISBN 0-7368-2020-5 (alk. paper)
  1. Light–Juvenile literature. 2. Shades and shadows–Juvenile literature. [1. Light. 2. Shadows.] I. Title. II. Science (Mankato, Minn.)
  QC360.R556 2003
  535'.4–dc21

                                                                      2003000922

Editorial Credits
Mary Lindeen, Editorial Director; Jennifer Van Voorst, Editor; Wanda Winch, Photo Researcher

Photo Credits
Cover: David Seawell/Corbis; Title Page: Jim Foell/Capstone Press; Page 2: BananaStock Ltd.; Page 3: Jim Foell/Capstone Press; Page 4: Lawrence Lawry/PhotoDisc; Page 5: Jim Foell/Capstone Press; Page 6: Jim Foell/Capstone Press; Page 7: Steve Cole/PhotoDisc; Page 8: Creatas; Page 9: Jim Foell/Capstone Press; Page 10: Comstock; Page 11: Jim Foell/Capstone Press; Page 12: Jim Foell/Capstone Press; Page 13: Vicky Kasala/PhotoDisc; Page 14: Creatas; Page 15: Jim Foell/Capstone Press; Page 16: Jim Foell/Capstone Press

1 2 3 4 5 6 08 07 06 05 04 03

Light and Shadow

by Susan Ring

Consultant: Dr. Paul Ohmann, Assistant Professor of Physics,
University of St. Thomas

Yellow Umbrella Books

an imprint of Capstone Press
Mankato, Minnesota

The sun gives us light.

Lamps give us light.

Candles give us light.

We get light in many ways.

Light can go through glass.

Light can even go through colored glass.

Light cannot go through a soccer ball.

Can you see the ball's shadow?

Light cannot go through me!

Can you see my shadow?

Sometimes a shadow is big.

Sometimes a shadow is small.

My shadow jumps with me.

My shadow runs with me.

What kind of shadow do you see here?

Words to Know/Index

Word Count: 82
Early-Intervention Level: 8